POQUOSON

This Book was

Generously Donated
by the

Poquoson
Kiwanis Club

In Honor of

Cat Clark

Animal Aid Society
of Hampton, Virginia

July 2021

minedition

North American edition published 2020 by minedition, New York

Text copyright © 2011 Brigitte Weninger
Illustrations copyright © 2011 Eve Tharlet
Coproduction with Michael Neugebauer Publishing Ltd., Hong Kong.
Rights arranged with "minedition ag", Zurich, Switzerland. All rights reserved.
This book, or parts thereof, may not be reproduced in any form without permission
in writing from the publisher.
The scanning, uploading and distribution of this book via the Internet or via any other
means without the permission of the publisher is illegal and punishable by law.
Please purchase only authorized electronic editions, and do not participate in or encourage
electronic piracy of copyrighted materials. Your support of the author's rights is appreciated.
Michael Neugebauer Publishing Ltd.,
19 West 21st Street, #1201, New York, NY 10010
e-mail: info@minedition.com
This book was printed in May 2020 at Hong Kong Discovery Printing Company Limited.
3/F., Blue Box Factory Building, 25 Hing Wo Street, Tin Wan, Aberdeen, Hong Kong, China
Typesetting in Icone
Library of Congress Cataloging-in-Publication Data available upon request.

ISBN 978-1-6626-5007-9
10 9 8 7 6 5 4 3 2 1
First Impression

For more information please visit our website: www.minedition.com

The Sharing Party

Brigitte Weninger

with pictures by Eve Tharlet

minedition

It was early in the Fall, and the apples were ripe.

Max Mouse was delighted and started painting a sign on a large piece of old cardboard. "What are you writing?" asked Henry Hedgehog. "It's an invitation to our friends," said Max.

"Join us for an Apple Party – this evening at Max's," read the young mouse. "Now I've got to pick the apples. But I won't be able to carry them myself. Will you help me?"

"Of course," Henry nodded. Max fetched two large bags, and they set off.

Max and Henry went deep into the woods.

"Wh... where's your apple tree?" asked Henry, anxiously.

"It's in a big clearing that only I know about," said Max.

"But – now I'll know it too," said Henry, confused.

"That's okay," said Max with a laugh. "We're friends, and friends share secrets!"

But when Max and Henry arrived at the clearing...

...not a single apple remained on the tree!

Max just stared up at the branches. "I don't understand," he said. "The day before yesterday all the branches were full of big, red apples!"

"Well, since then someone has been here and picked them all," sighed Henry. "Let's go, Max; we need to let everyone know that the apple party has been cancelled."

 They left, trudging sadly toward their friend Rico Dormouse's burrow.

When they reached Rico's burrow Henry said, "Look, Max, there are all the apples!"

Max, who was usually so cheerful, felt angry. "Hey," he said, "are you the one who took all the apples from the tree in the clearing?"

"Yes," Rico nodded proudly. "They were really heavy."

"And what are you going to do with them now?" Henry wanted to know.

"Eat them, of course," Rico replied.

"All by... by yourself?" Henry stuttered.

"Of course. I picked them all by myself," said Rico.

"That's just great," Max said angrily. "Well, from now on you can play all by yourself, too. We can't be friends with someone like you!"

Max Mouse stomped away as Henry trotted along beside him.

"He wasn't going to share them," Max kept muttering–and he sounded as if he might cry.

At home he pulled the invitation off the tree and said to Henry,
"Please tell the others that the apple party has been cancelled.
I want to be on my own. See you later!"

Max closed the door behind him, and Henry ran to see his friend
Molly Mole.

"That's so mean!" Molly said
when she heard the story. "And what
about our wonderful celebration?"

"Max cancelled it," Henry sighed. "No apples–no party."

"No!" shouted Molly. "We will still celebrate. We'll have a... a...
a pancake party! That's it! Yesterday I picked some wheat and ground
it into flour. I'd be happy to share it with everyone."

She got a little bag of flour from the larder, and then she and Henry
went down to the pond.

Freddy Frog was busy practicing jumps.

Henry called out, "Freddy! The apple
party has been cancelled because Rico
took all the apples for himself. But Molly is
sharing her flour with us, and we're going to
have a pancake party instead. Will you come?"

"Ribbit," answered the frog. "And Freddy share,
too!" He fetched a jug of water with an apricot
floating in it.

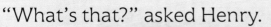

"What's that?" asked Henry.
"One apricot for five guests?"

But then Henry smelled the sweet scent
of apricot lemonade. "Hey, this smells wonderful!"

"Yummy, yummy!" nodded Freddy as they went off
to find Belinda Blackbird.

Belinda was very angry when her friends
told her about Rico and the apples.

"A tree in the woods belongs to everyone," she said.
"You can't just take all the fruit for yourself.
Poor Max, where is he?"

"At home," said Henry. "He doesn't know
anything about the pancake party."

"Then it will be a lovely surprise!" said Belinda.
"Come on—I'll just fill a basket with worms and..."

"YUK!" squealed Molly. "I don't want
a pancake with worms!"

"They're not for us, silly," laughed Belinda.
"They're for the chickens. I can swap
the worms for a couple of their eggs!"

As the group of friends got to Max's house there was already someone at the door.

"Rico, you greedy creature!" chirped Belinda angrily. "What are YOU doing here?"

"I'm so sorry, I don't know what I was thinking," said Rico. "It's not much fun eating all these apples on my own. Do you still want some?"

"Thank you, Rico," said Max. "It looks as if there will be an apple party, after all!"

"But we've brought everything for a pancake party," said Molly.

"Then we'll just have to have an apple pancake party," Rico said with a giggle. "I'll bet Max has a big pan and some butter."

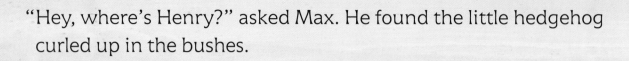

"Hey, where's Henry?" asked Max. He found the little hedgehog curled up in the bushes.

"Everyone has s... s... something to share," sobbed Henry. "I'm the o... o... only one with nothing!"

"That's not true," said Max, trying to comfort his friend. "Come out and have a look at yourself."

Henry was confused but crawled out from his hiding place.

"Your spikes are full of twigs," said Max, smiling. "We can use them to light our oven. Can you collect some more?"

Soon all six friends were busy. Molly and Freddy stirred the pancake batter, Belinda and Henry built the fire, Rico cut the apples into thin slices, and Max mixed up a huge pancake. He sang while he worked:

*"Sharing, sharing is such fun to do –
when we all share, there's always enough,
enough for me and you...
La-la-lalala..."*

"It's ready," said Max. "Now we just need a bit of magic..."

Max carefully sprinkled some sugar onto the pancake and then divided it into six equal pieces.

"What's that?" asked Henry.

"It's friendship powder," Max said with a wink. "With friendship powder, everything we eat together tastes even sweeter."

And then it was quiet until they had eaten up every last crumb. Rico sang softly to himself:

"Sharing, sharing, is such fun to do –
when we all share, there's always enough,
enough for me and you...
La-la-lalala..."

How do you make apple pancakes?

You'll find the recipe and much more on our website: www.minedition.com.

One more question to think about: How many slices did each of the six friends get from their big apple pancake?

What else can you share? Think about it—secrets, feelings, ideas, and fun!

What will YOU share?